*For Finn*
S. N.

*For Silas*
P. V.

*Thanks to Daryl*

PURRFECT!
TAMARIND BOOKS 978 1 870 51686 0

Published in Great Britain by Tamarind Books,
a division of Random House Children's Books
A Random House Group Company

This edition published 2008

1 3 5 7 9 10 8 6 4 2

Text copyright © Sarah Nash, 2008
Illustrations copyright © Pamela Venus, 2008

Set in Bembo MT School book

TAMARIND BOOKS
61–63 Uxbridge Road, London, W5 5SA

www.tamarindbooks.co.uk
www.kidsatrandomhouse.co.uk
www.rbooks.co.uk

Addresses for companies within The Random House Group Limited can be found at:
www.randomhouse.co.uk/offices.htm

THE RANDOM HOUSE GROUP Limited Reg. No. 954009

A CIP catalogue record for this book is available from the British Library.

Printed and bound in China

# Purrfect!

## Sarah Nash

*Illustrated by Pamela Venus*

Tamarind

"Tiger needs a wash,"
says Nana.

"Nana, look! My tiger's lost his stripes
in the washing machine," gasps Tyrone.
    "Ooops! I can't see them anywhere," says Nana.
    "Nana, what shall we do? Tiger MUST
have his stripes," squeaks Tyrone.

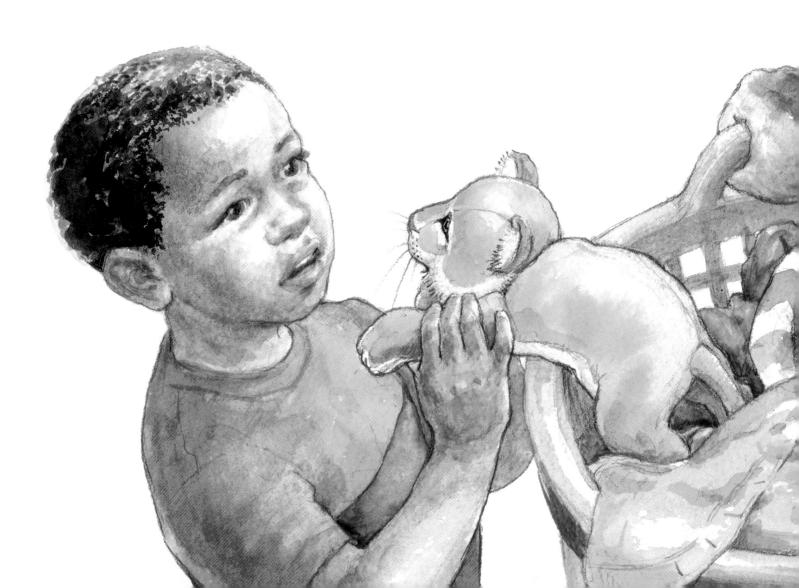

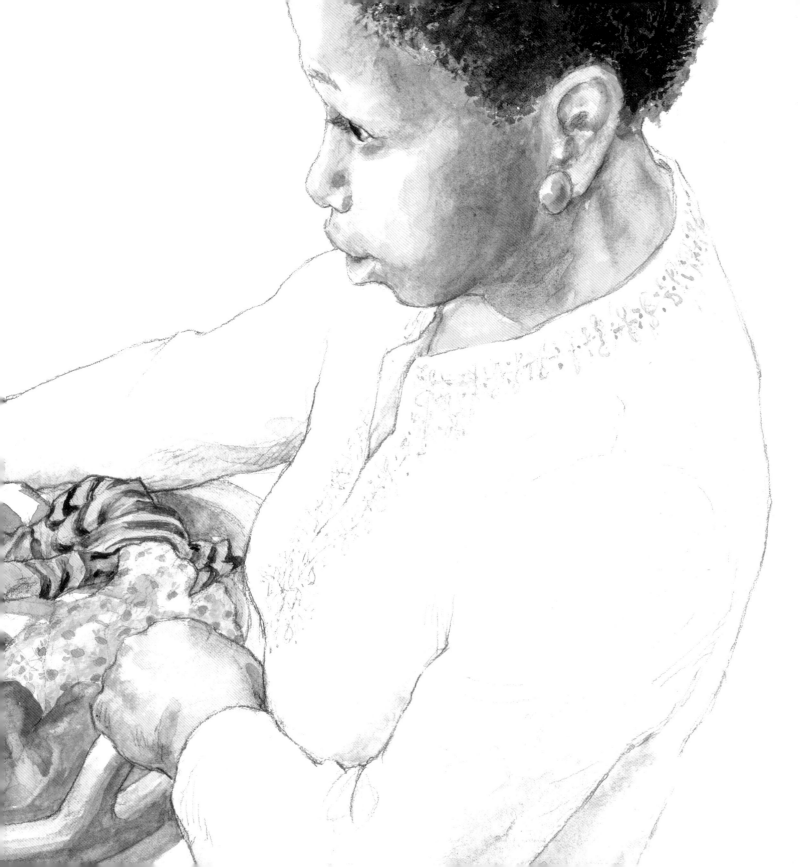

"Let's see if
we can find
him some,"
says Nana.

"Let's put him in these striped shadows,"
says Grandpa.

"Oh no, they're all gone,"
sighs Tyrone.

"Let's draw them on
with a pen," says Dad.

"Oh no, the rain's washing them off!" cries Tyrone.

"Let's put Poppy's hair bands round him," says Mum.

"Oh no, they fall off when we dance," laughs Tyrone.

"Let's sew them on," says Auntie.

"Ohhh NOOOOoooo!
You can't do that.

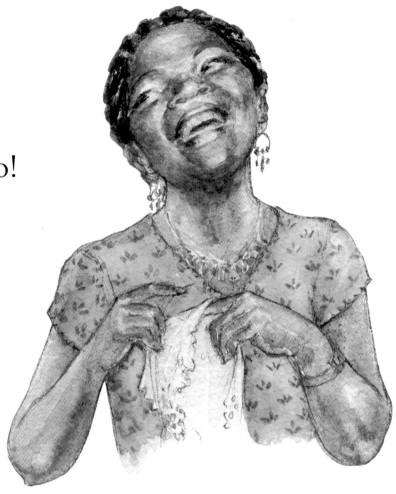

Tiger's frightened of
needles!" exclaims Tyrone.

"Could he be a tiger with no stripes?" asks Nana.

"Yes, but he likes wearing his stripes," says Tyrone.

"I know what we
can do. . ." says Nana.
"I will knit him a stripy suit.
Then he can wear his stripes
whenever he wants."

"And he can take them off when
he goes in the washing machine. . .

SO THEY DON'T GET LOST!" shouts Tyrone.

"How's that?" asks Nana.
    "Perfect!" says Tyrone.
    "Purr . . . fect!" says Tiger.

# Other Tamarind titles available:

## FOR READERS OF *PURRFECT!*

And Me!
Choices, Choices . . .
What Will I Be?
All My Friends
A Safe Place
Dave and the Tooth Fairy
Where's Gran?
Time for Bed
Time to Get Up
Giant Hiccups
Are We There Yet?
Mum's Late
I Don't Eat Toothpaste Anymore

## FOR TODDLERS

The Best Blanket
The Best Home
The Best Mum
The Best Toy

Let's Feed the Ducks
Let's Go to Bed
Let's Have Fun
Let's Go to Playgroup

## FOR OLDER READERS

Big Eyes, Scary Voice
The Dragon Kite
The Night the Lights Went Out
Princess Katrina and the Hair Charmer
South African Animals
Caribbean Animals
The Feather
The Bush
Marty Monster
Starlight
Dizzy's Walk
Boots for a Bridesmaid
Yohance and the Dinosaurs

## FOR BABIES

Baby Goes
Baby Plays
Baby Noises
Baby Finds

and if you are interested in
seeing the rest of our list,
please visit our website:
www.tamarindbooks.co.uk